FLY HIGH, LOLO

Written and illustrated
by Niki Daly

*For Mr Ben, who will soon
be reading on his own*

For further information,
write Catalyst Press, info@catalystpress.org.

Originally published in 2019 by Otter-Barry Books in Great Britain

FIRST EDITION 10 9 8 7 6 5 4 3 2 1

Library of Congress Control Number: 2022930558

Illustrated with digital art

Set in Maiandra GD

FLY HIGH,
LOLO

Written and illustrated
by Niki Daly

**CATALYST
PRESS**

Contents

Lolo and the Eagle

"Children!" said Miss Diaz. "This term
I would like us to do a play."

"Oh, Miss! Can there be gangsters?"
asked Tyrone.

"And cops!" shouted Ringo.

"Yes! Like on TV, who have tattoos and
cool stuff!" added Saleem.

"But what about us girls?" asked Lolo.

"Girls can also be cops!" replied Ringo.

"And gangsters!" said

Aziza, narrowing her eyes.

There was a lot of noise, with everyone talking at the same time. Lolo stayed quiet. She loved acting and plays. But she didn't like gangsters.

"Quiet now," said Miss Diaz. "I have a lovely story that we can act out. And there'll be a part for everyone."

Miss Diaz took out a book called *Fly, Eagle, Fly!* and started to read.

It was a wonderful story about a farmer finding an eagle chick and raising it among his chickens. One day a friend told him,

"This is not a chicken, it is an eagle!"

But the farmer would not believe him until the friend took the eagle into the mountains and set it free to fly as it was born to fly— high, high, high in the sky.

At the end of the story, Miss Diaz chose Mandla to play the farmer and Ringo to play his friend. There was a part for the farmer's wife and children, but just then the bell rang.

"We'll carry on when we next meet for drama," said Miss Diaz.

Lolo couldn't wait until the next drama class.

She told Mama and Gogo the story and how she was hoping to play the part of the eagle.

"Now, don't get your hopes up too high," said Gogo, "I'm sure there are many of your friends who would like to play such a good part."

But Lolo couldn't help dreaming of herself as the eagle, flying high in the sky...

and landing on
the edge of steep cliffs.

But just before the next drama class, Lolo caught a cold and had to miss school. And by the time she got back to school, Dana Rose, who did ballet and could do graceful leaps and land as softly as a feather, had been chosen for the part.

"Don't worry, Lolo," said Miss Diaz. "There are lots of parts as chickens."

So that's what Lolo did at each rehearsal, along with ten other chickens. They all went *cluck, cluck, cluck...*

while Dana Rose flew about the stage on tippy-toes, with wings outstretched.

15

At last the play was ready to be performed. But first costumes and stage sets had to be made.

Belinda from the art center got her older students to help build a hut and paint a beautiful mountain backdrop.

Then they were ready to go.

Lolo looked splendid in her chicken costume with its red wings and tail feathers.

The play went beautifully. The farmer and his friend made everyone laugh, as the chickens huddled together, going *cluck, cluck, cluck.*

Thabu, who was the cockerel, even let out a mighty crow.

Cock-a-doodle-doo!

Dana Rose was marvelous as the eagle, but...

right at the end, when she was supposed to fly, she fell in a heap of feathers and couldn't get up.

EEEK!

The eagle had twisted an ankle!

The audience gasped and the curtains closed. Backstage, Miss Diaz's boyfriend, a doctor, opened the school first-aid kit and bandaged Dana Rose's ankle.

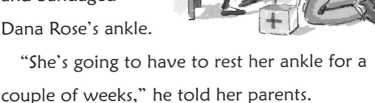

"She's going to have to rest her ankle for a couple of weeks," he told her parents.

The following day, with one more show to go, Miss Diaz asked if anyone wanted to play the eagle. No one wanted to twist their ankle so there were no hands... until Lolo put up her hand.

"Wonderful, Lolo," said Miss Diaz. "You've saved the play!"

And Lolo certainly did! The audience cheered as Lolo swooped and dived over the painted mountain tops, while all the cast sang, "Fly, Eagle, Fly!"

When Dana Rose returned to school,
she met Lolo in the playground and said,
"I heard that you made a great eagle."

Lolo smiled shyly and then she lifted her
head and said, "Let's fly together!"

From her classroom window, Miss Diaz
saw two proud eagles swooping around the
playground—flying in wider and wider circles.
"Fly, Eagles, Fly!" whispered Miss Diaz, and
then she got ready for the next drama class.

Lolo and the Teen Queen

Lolo was looking
in the mirror.

"*I wish I had long
braids like Zinzi,*" she
thought. She looked
some more and added,
"*And long silky eyelashes like Aiesha.*"

"I don't like your nose,"
said Lolo, pulling a funny
face. "And your mouth
looks like a little plum."

Lolo wished she could look like one of those models who advertised lipstick and perfume in Mama's magazines.

Lolo could see a tube of lipstick sticking out of Mama's make-up bag. Next to the bag lay Mama's dangly earrings.

When Lolo came to the breakfast table she did not look at all like a Lolo ready for school.

"Lolo?" said Gogo. "What have you been up to?"

"I've made myself beautiful," replied Lolo.

"You are already beautiful, sweetie," said Gogo. "Besides, lipstick and glitter doesn't make anyone beautiful inside."

"But I want to be beautiful *outside!*" said Lolo.

"You are beautiful on the inside *and* on the outside," said Gogo. "Now go and wash your face and put your mama's earrings back. You can't go to school looking like Miss World."

At school, Lolo kept staring at her friends.

Lindiwe Majola,
with her long braids...

Sisipho Dlomo, with her
beautiful smile and teeth
like pearls...

Beauty Mabedla, who wasn't
very beautiful but who
had a beautiful name...

and Koos, the new boy,
who had eyes as blue as
a blue-blue sky.

It made Lolo feel miserable, looking at her beautiful friends.

"Anything wrong, Lolo?" asked Mrs. McKenzie.

"No," said Lolo.

But something WAS wrong.

"Lolo," said Mama, "I haven't seen that happy Lolo face for days now. Tell me what's the matter."

Lolo poured her heart out to Mama.

And when Mama heard how Lolo was feeling, she held her in her arms and told her a story....

"Do you know the Old Aunty who lives down the road?" said Mama.

"Yes," said Lolo.
She often saw the old lady,
who was as gray as
a rain cloud and as wrinkled
as a scrunched-up paper bag.

"Well, can you imagine that
she was once Miss Soweto?"
said Mama.

Lolo couldn't imagine
the sweet old lady having ever
been a beauty queen.

"See?" said Mama,
"Beauty on the outside
doesn't last forever. But
when a person has beautiful
thoughts and feelings, it lasts
a whole lifetime.

What do you think?"

Lolo thought about it before she went to sleep.

But she wondered if what Mama said was true, or if Mama was just trying to make her feel better.

Next day, when Gogo caught Lolo looking at herself in the mirror, she said, "Hey, Miss! Stop looking at yourself and come with me."

Gogo always found nice things to do. And it was fun being together. *Yebo!* Much better than thinking about beauty queens and who had the most beautiful nose or toes in the world.

"You're looking happy today, Lolo,"
said Mrs. McKenzie, as the children came
into the classroom.

34

"I have exciting news," announced Mrs. McKenzie. "Tomorrow is Tuesday, when we invite a guest to the school. My niece, Jacqueline, who has just won the Miss Teen Beauty Competition, has agreed to visit us!"

A buzz of excitement filled the classroom.

Lolo had seen Jacqueline McKenzie on television and she was stunningly beautiful.

The following morning, Lolo and two other girls were asked to welcome Miss Teen. And what an arrival! There were cameras and reporters around her, shouting out questions.

Miss Teen put on a big smile for the cameras but she didn't even say hello to the welcoming team.

Quietly, they led her to a packed school hall.

Mr. Hendricks, the headteacher, welcomed Miss Teen in his booming voice that never needed a microphone. *"Children, I have the pleasure of welcoming Miss Teen to the school. I'm sure she has something important to share with us."*

Then he handed the mic to Miss Teen, but no one could hear her. "Switch it on," whispered Mr. Hendricks.

"This stupid thing needs a new battery!" she said sharply.

And then she did something that made the children go...

40

She threw the mic on the floor!

"Will someone please shut those stupid curtains!" she demanded. "The sun is blinding me! And YOU in front—stop swinging your leg around! *It's sooo distraaacting!*"

Mr. Hendricks picked up the mic, switched
it on, then handed it back to Miss Teen. But
she was just awful! She spoke *all* about herself
and how she
planned to become
Miss World.
Even when
children asked
important questions
about starving people
and protecting animals
she turned the question back to herself.

"I want to be a role model for all beautiful
little girls," she told them.

Back in class, Mrs. McKenzie looked upset.

"I must apologize for my niece's behavior," she said. "I think she must be very stressed by all the attention she's getting."

"Don't worry, Miss," said Thabo, "I'm always stressed on Tuesdays."

"Oh dear! Why?" asked Mrs. McKenzie.

"Because this is the day my dad makes my lunch," said Thabo.

Everyone laughed. Then the bell rang and they *all* wanted to see what Thabo's dad had made him—*a spaghetti sandwich!*

On the way home from school Lolo walked past Old Aunty. She was sweeping her path, but she looked up and gave Lolo a smile that wrinkled her face even more and made her eyes sparkle.

"Oh, little one, I've seen you pass by every day, and I have something I want you to have. Just wait here!" said Old Aunty. She tottered inside, returning with a plastic bag.

"Open it when you get home!" said Old Aunty and she patted Lolo's hand.

"Thank you, Old Aunty," said Lolo, and she hurried home.

"Let's see what Old Aunty has given you," said Gogo.

Well, what was inside made Lolo and Gogo gasp!

"Oh, Lolo! It's a beauty queen's crown!" cried Gogo, and she carefully placed it on Lolo's head.

"Now go and look at yourself," said Gogo.

Lolo's face lit up as brightly as the shiny jewels in the crown.

"So, how do you feel?" asked Gogo.

 Lolo smiled a beautiful smile, a smile that comes from feeling very, very happy deep inside.

Lolo's First Date

Mama was talking to Gogo about someone
at Mama's work.

Lolo was listening.

"It's Sam this and Sam that,"
said Gogo. "When are we
going to meet this Sam?"

"This weekend," said Mama. "I'm going
on a date with him on Saturday afternoon."

It was the first time that Lolo had heard of
Mama going on a date. And she knew what
a date was. It was when someone you like,
and who likes you back, asks you out. Lolo
frowned. Who was this Sam?

47

Lolo tried to imagine
what Sam might look
like. The handsome TV
weatherman?

Maybe Bro Matt,
the friendly owner of
Bro Matt's Coffee Shop?

Or, what about
the Black Panther?

On Saturday morning Mama was not doing Saturday morning chores, like cleaning the house and going to the shops.

Instead, she was in her room, trying on all her dresses

and doing fancy styles with her hair.

"How do I look in this dress?" she asked
Gogo, after trying on five dresses.

"Just fine," said Gogo. "You're not going to
meet Prince Harry, are you?"

Lolo felt ignored.

She did a headstand.

She pummeled a cushion.

She jumped up and
down on the bed.

She let out the biggest yawn ever.

Still Mama kept on fussing—now over shoes. "What do you think about these shoes, Lolo?" asked Mama. Lolo rolled her eyes and left the room.

"Oh, Lolooo!" Mama called after her.

Lolo was fed up. How could Mama go out with this Sam and not her! Especially if they were going somewhere nice to eat, or to see a film.

Lolo folded her arms and put on her "I'm-not-happy" face.

"Why the face?" asked Gogo.

"It's not fair!" said Lolo. "Mama's going on a date without me."

"Oh, Lolo," said Gogo gently. "Your Mama needs to have some time on her own. She's still young and pretty, and it's nice to be paid attention by someone who thinks you're special."

"Well, *I'm* special, and *no one* is paying me *any* attention today!" Lolo complained.

"When you grow up you will have lots of dates," said Gogo. "Then who's going to keep me company?"

But Lolo wasn't going to change her mind—unfair is unfair!

At last Mama was dressed for her date.

"You look a million dollars, Sisi," said Gogo.

Lolo noticed Mama was smelling very nice too, but she didn't say anything. Sulking was all she could do. And she planned to keep it up until the very last minute.

Yebo! When Mama and her Sam walked out of the front door, they would feel her sulk like pins in their backs!

Mama ran to the front door.

"Hi, Sam. Come in," cooed Mama.

Lolo hid behind Gogo, but when she peeped out...

Sam didn't look at all like anyone she had imagined!

"This is Lolo," said Mama.

"Pleased to meet you, Lolo," said Sam.
"Your mother has told me a lot about you."
And then he smiled! Such a smile that Lolo
just had to smile back.

"I brought these for you," he said, handing
Lolo a bunch of flowers.

Lolo felt too shy to open her mouth.

"Come, Lolo," said Gogo. "We'll put these
in a vase."

"So, what do you think of Sam?" Gogo whispered.

"He's OK," whispered Lolo. "But he's not like the Black Panther."

"That's true," whispered Gogo, "but we can't all be super-heroes. Besides, he looks like a sweetie to me."

"We're going now," called Mama.

Gogo and Lolo joined them in the sitting room. Mama kissed Lolo goodbye.

"Have a nice time!" said Gogo, as they walked to the door.

But just before it opened, Sam turned and said...

"Want to come
with us, Lolo?"

Lolo couldn't
believe her ears!
In a tick she had on
her trainers and her
Mr. Smiley backpack.

"Have a good time," called Gogo as they
drove away. And that's exactly the time they
had!

First, they had
a yummy lunch.

And after that,
Lolo went on
a bumper car.

And then Lolo had her face
painted like a butterfly.

And last of all, they went
for a walk along the beach.
Except...

it wasn't a clean beach. There was litter all over the place—straws, plastic bottle caps, cigarette stubs and plastic carrier-bags rolling along white sand.

"What a mess," said Sam.

"Disgusting," said Mama.

"I'm going to clean it up," said Lolo,
running after a drifting bag.

"Grab one for me!" called Sam.

"Me too!" added Mama.

Soon their bags were bulging with litter.
But there was still a lot more lying around.

"We can't clean it all up," said Mama.

"Mrs. McKenzie said that if we all do our bit, we'll be able to clean the whole world," said Lolo.

"Maybe we can make this our special Saturday 'beach-clean' date," said Sam. "Would you like that, Lolo?"

Lolo smiled, and put her foot down on a plastic bag before it blew into the sea.

"Yes please!" she said.

Lolo's Recycled Christmas Tree

When Lolo learned about the terrible effect that pollution has on nature, she decided to pick up litter on her way back from school. If there was a bin along the way, she threw it in. But often the bin was overflowing, so she'd take it home in the plastic bag she started carrying with her.

"Lolo! Are you are turning our house into a rubbish dump?" complained Gogo.

"No, Gogo, I'm recycling," said Lolo.

"Recycling, recycling! That's all I hear these days," said Gogo. "When I was your age there wasn't all this plastic stuff lying around—like it's raining plastic!"

"Mrs. McKenzie says that we can help by recycling and not using so much plastic," said Lolo.

"Well, that's why I still use my shopping basket," said Gogo. "Besides, it's easier to carry home on my head when my hands are full." Lolo was amazed that Gogo was able to carry heavy loads balanced on her head.

Gogo told her that was how everyone carried their goods when she was young. She said it was the best way, because it kept you standing up tall rather than slouching.

By the end of term, before the summer holidays and Christmas, Lolo had collected soft drink cans, colorful bottle caps, plastic foam tubs and anything that sparkled and looked interesting. She had seen how clever people turned junk into things they could sell.

Plastic bottles and tins could
be made into flowers.

Tin cans and foam trays
could be turned into
sculptures...

and bottle caps and
plastic foam tubs could
become mobiles.

Lolo loved the long summer holidays, except that Mama was hardly ever home  because she had to work longer hours before Christmas. "Sisi, you'll wear yourself out," Gogo told Mama.

"I have to earn a bit more money, Ma," said Mama, "You know how expensive it is at this time of the year."

"Well, we don't have to have all the nice things we like," said Gogo. "I can do without my biscuits with tea."

"And I can go without my special coffee," said Mama, "but we must make things nice for Lolo."

As usual, Lolo heard it all! And it made her feel sad. So she went to her room to have a good think.

And then she remembered her holiday project.

First she went across the road to Tata
Mabusa, who had a half-dead tree in his
front garden.

"*Molo*, Tata," said Lolo.

"*Molo*, Lolo," replied the old man. "What
can I do for you?"

"May I have a branch from your old tree, please?" asked Lolo.

"You may have the whole tree, if you like," said Tata Mabusa. "It's as old and bent as I am!" he joked.

Now Lolo was ready to start. First, she washed everything she planned to use and let it dry in the sun.

"Hey, sweetie," called Gogo. "What's going on?"

"You'll see," Lolo called back.

Bottle tops with little beads became Christmas bells. She cut stars and flowers from colored bits of plastic. A plastic foam tub and a scrap of bubble wrap turned into a Christmas Angel.

Sam came by and helped cut out some Christmas decorations from tin cans. But there was still more to do!

"I need my Christmas tree to stand up straight," said Lolo.

Sam thought for a while, then snapped his fingers.

"Sand!" he said, "We'll fill an empty paint tin with sand and stick it in."

Immediately, Sam went off and returned with a bag of sand and some empty tin cans. They stuck the branch in a can and then decorated it.

"Beautiful!" called Gogo.

"Yes, Lolo," said Sam. "Your idea is too good for just one Christmas tree. Let's make more! I bet we can sell them at the market and that will give you some holiday money."

And that's what they did. They even painted the branches from Tata Mabusa's old tree in Christmas colors—red, gold and green.

Every tree was sold!

And the money?

Yebo! For Christmas, Lolo bought Gogo her special biscuits and Mama her special coffee. And Lolo still had some holiday money left over for herself.

And Sam?

Well, Sam was delighted with his recycled
paper-bag hat...

made with love by Lolo.

Niki Daly

has won many awards for his work.
His groundbreaking *Not So Fast, Songololo*, winner
of a US Parent's Choice Award, paved the way
for post-apartheid South African children's books.
Among his many books, *Once Upon a Time* was
an Honor Winner in the US Children's Africana
Book Awards and *Jamela's Dress* was chosen by the
ALA as a Notable Children's Book and by Booklist as
one of the Top 10 African American Picture Books—
it also won both the Children's Literature Choice
Award and the Parents' Choice Silver Award.
Niki wrote and illustrated the picture book
Surprise! Surprise! for Otter-Barry Books.
He lives with his wife, the author and illustrator
Jude Daly, in South Africa.

 Collect all the Lolo books!